Meier

271-7316

DANNY LOVES
A HOLIDAY

DANNY LOVES
A HOLIDAY

Sydney Taylor

illustrated by Gail Owens

E. P. DUTTON   NEW YORK

Library of Congress Cataloging in Publication Data

Taylor, Sydney, date   Danny loves a holiday.

Summary: Throughout the year Danny and his family celebrate
Rosh Hashanah, Yom Kippur, Sukkot, Hanukkah, Hamishah Asar
Bishevat, Purim, Passover, Lag ba-Omer, Shavuot, and the Sabbath.
[1. Jews—Rites and ceremonies—Fiction. 2. Fasts and
feasts—Judaism—Fiction. 3. Jews in the United States—
Fiction] I. Owens, Gail. II. Title.
PZ7.T2184Dan 1980 [Fic] 80-17065 ISBN: 0-525-28510-5

Published in the United States by E. P. Dutton, a Division
of Elsevier-Dutton Publishing Company, Inc., New York

Published simultaneously in Canada by Clarke,
Irwin & Company Limited, Toronto and Vancouver

Editor: Ann Durell   Designer: Stacie Rogoff

Printed in the U.S.A.   First Edition
10 9 8 7 6 5 4 3 2 1

CONTENTS

Danny loves a holiday
'Cause holidays are fun.
Hardly has one ended when
He wants another one.

If it were up to Danny,
He'd jump with joy and cheer.
Let's have a happy holiday
Each day throughout the year!

Come Blow Your Horn

Danny paraded before Mommy. He was all dressed up. From the hat on his curly head, down to the shiny brown shoes, everything he was wearing today had been bought especially for Rosh Hashanah (the New Year).

"I'm all brand-new!" he said proudly.

Mommy shook a finger at him. "Not only on the outside, Danny. We should feel brand-new on the inside too. You see, on Rosh Hashanah, everything begins all over again. We are sorry for the bad things we did last year, and we ask God to forgive us. We're very glad that we have an-

other chance. And we must promise ourselves that we'll try awfully hard to do better in the new year."

Danny marched over to the mirror and admired himself.

"Come, Danny, it's time to go to services," Mommy reminded.

The synagogue was crowded with people. Danny's brown eyes searched the wide room.

"There's Grandpa and Daddy!" he whispered excitedly.

His new shoes went *squeak, squeak* as he tiptoed down the aisle.

The sound of praying filled the synagogue. Danny watched Grandpa rock himself back and forth, back and forth, as he chanted. Now it was loud, now soft. It's like a song, Danny said to himself. He wished he were old enough to read from the Hebrew prayer book and sing out loud.

He looked around. All the men had prayer shawls, and they wore skullcaps on their heads. Some of the people's faces are so sad looking, he thought. I guess that's because today they're asking God to forgive them.

The wooden bench felt hard. Danny twisted against the straight back. All the singsongy chanting made him sleepy. First he rubbed his eyes with his fists. Then he pushed his tongue against the loose tooth in the front of his mouth and wiggled it in and out.

Grandpa gave Danny a nudge. "Look!" he whispered. Danny sat upright, craning his neck. On the platform, the rabbi was holding a large, curved, grayish thing to his lips.

"That's a shofar, Danny," Grandpa said.

"It looks like a cow's horn, Grandpa."

"No, It's made from the horn of a ram."

"Is he going to blow it now, Grandpa?"

"Shhh!" Grandpa held up a warning finger. "Right now, Danny. Listen!"

Ti-KEE-yoo! Tra-ta-ta-ta-ta! Ti-KEE-yoo!

What a strange, exciting sound! Danny gave a little shiver. Daddy had told him that in olden days they always blew a shofar when something important was happening.

"Grandpa," he said, "is only the rabbi allowed to blow the shofar, or can anybody?"

Grandpa peered down at him. "Would you like to blow the shofar, Danny?"

"Oh, could I? Could I?"

"Shhh! We'll see. Afterward—maybe."

The services went on and on but now Danny had the shofar to think about. The chanting was growing louder and even sadder than before. Several times more, the shofar was blown. Each time, Danny trembled with eagerness to blow the horn all by himself.

Then came the moment when the ark of the Torah was opened and all could see the Holy Books. Grandpa and Daddy and all the men pulled their prayer shawls over their heads. Now Danny thought he could hear crying mixed up with the praying. It made him want to cry too. He sent his prayer up to heaven. "I promise from now on I'll be good. And I'll do everything Mommy and Daddy tell me. . . ."

Finally the services came to an end. Everyone went about wishing everybody else a good year. "Grandpa, now can I blow the shofar?" Danny kept asking. And always Grandpa replied, "In a little while, Danny—maybe."

At long last, most of the people had gone. Danny held on eagerly to Mommy and Daddy as Grandpa talked to the rabbi. The rabbi smiled. He put the precious shofar into Danny's hands. "Here, Danny," he said, "maybe you can do better than I."

Danny blew and blew, but the only thing that came out was the sound of his breath. Where was the strange music?

Grandpa laughed. "Oh, you'll have to blow much harder than that!"

Danny took a deep breath and blew hard. Still, all that came out was—*pff . . . ff . . . ffff!*

Danny's lips pushed out stubbornly. What was the matter with that old horn, anyway? He'd give it one last try. He breathed in—a great—big—giant breath. Then he blew with all his might. His cheeks puffed out. His face grew fiery red. He felt as if his lungs were bursting. But all that anybody heard was—*pff* . . . *ff* . . . *ffff!*

"It's no use, Grandpa," complained Danny. "It just won't blow."

"Well, don't feel so bad," Grandpa said. "It's very hard to blow a shofar. It takes lots and lots of practice."

As Danny handed the shofar back to the rabbi, something inside it rattled. Wonderingly, the rabbi shook the shofar. *Rattle, rattle!*

"Hmm. There must be something inside," he said.

He tipped the shofar over into the palm of his hand. A small, shiny piece of white came tumbling out. The rabbi stared down at it.

"It's a tooth! A little tooth!" he cried out in surprise.

Swiftly Danny's tongue went exploring. Sure enough! Where his wiggly tooth had been, there was now an empty space!

"It's mine! That's my tooth!" he shouted, gleefully. "I blew so hard, I blew it right into the shofar!"

Everyone fell to laughing. "Well, rabbi," Grandpa said, "lots of people can blow a shofar, but my little grandson Danny is the first one to make it rattle!"

A Million Zillion Years

"You make up with Bobby yet, Danny?" asked Daddy.

"Nope! I'm not going to make up with him for a million zillion years!"

"That's a pretty long time," Daddy said, smiling.

"I don't care!" Danny burst out. "Bobby's mean! He's just as mean as he can be!"

"Oh, I don't know about that."

"Oh, yes he is!"

"Now, now, Danny, haven't you ever been a little mean yourself sometime?"

"Not like him. I always let him play with my things. And yesterday he wouldn't let me play with his sailboat."

"He'd only just gotten it, hadn't he?"

"But I only wanted it for a little while. Just so I could sail it in the bathtub. But he was mean! He wouldn't let me. He grabbed it right out of my hands, and then he socked me on the head with it—hard!"

"Well, Danny, sometimes when people are angry, they do something that isn't very nice. But people don't really want to be mean, Danny, and they're always sorry afterwards. Can't you forgive Bobby?"

Danny stamped his foot. "No! And anyway, he's not sorry!"

"How do you know?"

"Because if he was, he'd come and say so."

"Well, Danny, it's very hard to say I'm sorry. Couldn't you help by letting him know that you're not really mad at him anymore?"

"No, I'm not going to!" Danny muttered stubbornly.

Daddy thought a moment. Then he spoke quietly. "Yom Kippur starts tonight. Do you know what Yom Kippur means?"

Danny looked up in surprise. Why was Daddy talking about Yom Kippur all of a sudden? Well, anyhow, he was glad they weren't going to talk about Bobby anymore. He sighed. He and Bobby used to have lots of fun together.

"Well, Danny, do you?" Daddy asked again.

"Uh-huh. I know. That's the day we fast."

"And why do we fast?"

"To make up for being bad the whole year," Danny answered promptly.

Daddy shook his head. "That's only partly right. Yom Kippur is much more than that. The name tells you why. Yom Kippur is Hebrew for Day of Atonement. *Atonement* means to make up, just like you said, Danny. But we make up by doing more than just fasting.

"Ever since Rosh Hashanah began ten days ago, we've been going over in our minds all the wrong things we did during the whole year. We feel very unhappy about them, and on Yom Kippur we try to show God how truly sorry we are. We do this in several ways. First, we fast. Then we pray in the synagogue all day, and in our prayers we ask for God's forgiveness. Also, we promise to give to charity so that we can help those who are in need.

"Now God listens to us, and He is willing to forgive. But He wants us to be just as willing to do the same for each other. On Yom Kippur, we are asked to forgive not only our friends, but even our enemies, no matter how much they have hurt us. God wants us to begin the new year with love in our hearts, Danny, not hate."

Daddy stopped speaking. A great big, empty silence filled the room. Danny hung his head. He couldn't bear to meet Daddy's eyes. His chest felt funny, as if he couldn't breathe. There was a lump growing in his throat, too. Daddy's voice had been soft and gentle. He hadn't scolded, and yet Danny felt ashamed. This was because in his heart he knew that he deserved a scolding.

Slowly, Danny walked towards the door. "I guess I'll go out," he mumbled. The door closed quietly behind him.

Down the stairs Danny went, dragging his feet. Down the stairs and out into the street. He didn't have far to go.

Bobby's house was just around the corner. Danny halted for just a second; then, lifting his head high, he marched bravely ahead.

As he rounded the block, he saw Bobby on the porch of his house. He was standing with one hand behind his back and looking straight at him. Danny's heart began to beat fast.

"Hello, Danny!" Bobby called out, scrambling down the steps towards him. "I was just coming over to your house." He sounded extra cheerful.

Danny blurted out, "Bobby, I'm not mad anymore. And anyway, I shouldn't have tried to take
your boat away. I don't blame you for socking
me."

"Gee, Danny." Bobby sort of hunched up his
shoulders. "I'm awful sorry about yesterday. I
didn't mean to hit you." Quickly his arm came
from behind his back. He had his sailboat! He
held it out to Danny. "Here, Danny, want to
play with it? You can keep it till tomorrow if you
want."

Danny turned the boat round and round in his hand. It had such a smooth shape, and its white sail shone in the sunshine. It was nifty! And now Bobby was letting him play with it! Gee, Bobby is a swell friend, he thought.

Bobby grinned at him, and Danny felt his heart grow big and light. He put his arm around Bobby's shoulder. Together they strolled back to Danny's house.

"Gee, I'm glad it's Yom Kippur," Danny suddenly shouted. "I could never wait a million zillion years!"

"Huh?" Bobby looked wonderingly at Danny.

Danny bubbled over with joy and laughter. "Oh, come on, Bobby! Let's go sail your boat in my bathtub."

And they raced each other up the stairs.

The Old Etrog

Danny hippety-hopped over to Daddy and Grandpa. Together they stood in Grandpa's backyard, admiring the little sukkah (wooden hut). The walls looked snug and light. The roof was lightly covered with fresh green branches.

"Grandpa," Danny said, "this sukkah is like a real house."

"When the Jews left Egypt and wandered in the desert, they lived in little sukkahs like this," Grandpa said. "They didn't have time to build regular houses."

Grandma came out and looked. "Oh, my! That's the nicest sukkah we ever had!" she exclaimed.

"That's because Danny helped us this year," said Grandpa.

Danny felt very proud. "I sure wish the sukkah could stay here forever," he said.

"It'll be here for the whole Sukkot holiday. That's nine days, anyway," said Daddy.

Danny looked up at the sky. "Gosh, Grandma, suppose it starts raining tonight. Just when we're eating the first meal in the sukkah!"

"So we'll have a little more soup in the plates," Grandma replied, laughing.

"Now let's take the flowers and fruits and vegetables, and decorate the sukkah," suggested Daddy.

"Fruits and vegetables!" Danny chuckled.

"Yes, Danny. Sukkot is thanksgiving for the harvest. So we decorate with God's growing things," explained Grandpa. "That reminds me," he added, "I got an extra fine lulav this year."

"That's the palm branch, isn't it?" Danny said.

"Yes. It has three twigs of myrtle and two branches of willow tied to it. The Bible tells us that on Sukkot, we must hold the lulav and etrog

together and say a prayer. Then we shake the lulav in all directions to show that God is everywhere."

"Why do they call it etrog, Grandpa?" asked Danny. "It looks like a lemon."

"It's really a citron. It comes from Israel."

"Grandpa is very fond of his etrog," Grandma said with a smile. "He's had it for more years than I can remember. He'd rather use the old etrog than buy a new one each year."

"May I see it, Grandpa?"

"You saw it last year. Besides, it's in the kitchen cabinet. And anyway, we have to decorate the sukkah now."

As soon as Grandpa and Daddy were busy with the decorating, Danny slipped off to the kitchen. "Grandma, may I see the etrog?"

So Grandma put the etrog into Danny's hand. He turned it round and round. "It's bigger than a lemon. But it doesn't smell like one."

"There can't be much smell left in it by now, Danny," Grandma said. "A new etrog has a pleasant, spicy odor. Well, I'd better go out and sweep the sukkah. With Grandpa and Daddy decorating, the place must be a mess." Grandma sailed out of the kitchen.

Danny rolled the etrog back and forth across the table. Then he picked it up and shook it. I wonder what's inside, he said to himself. Tiptoeing over to the kitchen drawer, he took out a small knife. He tried to cut into the etrog, but the knife kept bouncing off.

He tried a can opener. Then scissors. He sawed, he fiddled, he scraped, he jabbed, he hacked. He couldn't even make a scratch.

Danny's eyes went roaming round the room. He spied Grandma's big wooden mallet. I guess I'll try that, he decided. Picking up the mallet, he raised it high. Down it came! Bang! Socko! A teeny clip of yellow flew off! "It's hard as a rock!!" He grunted.

"Danny! What are you doing with my etrog?"

It was Grandpa! His face was very stern. Danny's heart thumped. Now I'll catch it, he thought.

"Gee, Grandpa," he stammered. "I . . . I just . . . wanted—to see inside. . . ."

Without a word, Grandpa took the etrog from Danny. He stared down at the chipped spot and sighed. Gently his fingers smoothed it.

The room was very still. Danny didn't know what to say. He felt awful. Finally Grandpa spoke. "There's really nothing much to see. It's pure white inside." Grandpa's face was no longer angry. "Danny, this etrog has been around a long, long time," he said. "It's grown very, very hard. You can chop away at it. You can scratch it a little, but you can't break it. And it's just the same with a person's faith in God, Danny. Enemies may scratch and tear at it. They may leave their marks on it; but like this etrog, it grows strong and hard."

Grandpa's voice sounded proud. His face seemed lighted up.

Danny didn't understand. "Grandpa, you mean I'm hard, like the etrog?" he asked.

Grandpa tapped Danny on the head with the etrog. "Yes, Danny," he answered, "especially in the noodle!"

Hannah's Seventh Son

Miss Sturm looked around at the scrubbed, shiny faces of her Sunday school class. "We need a little boy for the Hanukkah play this year," she announced. "Now, let's see—who's the littlest one here?"

All the children pointed to Danny. "Danny! Danny's the littlest," they cried.

"Would you like the part, Danny?" Miss Sturm asked.

Danny's big brown eyes opened wide. Acting in a play! Oh boy! He nodded his head eagerly.

For the first time in his whole life, Danny was really glad he was the littlest.

"Now, class," Miss Sturm went on, "I want to tell you something about Hanukkah, the Festival of Lights.

"Long, long ago, Antiochus, king of Syria, came with a mighty army and took Palestine away from the Jews. He would not allow them to pray to God. He turned the Holy Temple in Jerusalem into a place for the worship of pagan gods. He tried to force the Jews to give up their religion. If they refused, he killed them.

"But there was one man, Judah Maccabee, who was not afraid. He said to the people, 'If we all get together, we'll be strong enough to fight. Join with me, and we'll drive the Syrians out of our land.'

"And all the brave young men gathered around Judah Maccabee. For three long years they fought, till at last they won. Jerusalem was theirs once more! Joyfully, the high priests returned to the Holy Temple to relight the golden, seven-branched menorah. Alas, they could find only one jug of oil. This would last for just one day. Then—lo and behold—a miracle happened! The light kept burning eight full days—enough time for fresh oil to be prepared.

"Though all this happened over two thousand

years ago, we have never forgotten. Every Hanukkah, we light the menorahs in our homes for eight days. We rejoice and give presents to one another, and sing songs to remind us.

"There are a number of legends about Hanukkah. One wonderful story tells about Hannah and her seven sons, who gave up their lives rather than give up their religion. I am very pleased that the older boys and girls have chosen this story for the Hanukkah play this year. It should be a good show. And Danny"—Miss Sturm smiled down on him—"will be Hannah's youngest son."

All week long, Danny rehearsed the play. He spoke the words and did exactly as Miss Sturm directed, but he felt troubled. Why did Hannah's sons have to die without fighting back? If somebody wants to kill you, you have to fight back, even if he is bigger than you. That's what Judah Maccabee did. He didn't just stand around and let that nasty old Antiochus get the best of him!

Each time they practiced the scene where Hannah's sons were lined up before Antiochus, Danny felt proud when they stubbornly refused to do the king's bidding. But when they let themselves be taken away to their doom, he grew more and more unhappy.

Finally, the afternoon of the play arrived. Danny felt all jumpy inside. He wiggle-waggled as Miss Sturm fitted him into his costume and put on his makeup. She patted him on the head encouragingly. "Now you look exactly like Hannah's youngest son—the bravest of all her seven children."

The curtain went up and the show began. The audience listened, spellbound, as one by one the sons were dragged off to torture and death. Now it was Danny's turn to face the tyrant.

"My child," the king said in a wheedling voice, "give up being a Jew, and I will make you rich and honored by all."

"Never!" the boy cried.

In vain did Antiochus plead with Hannah. "Persuade thy last remaining son to yield."

But Hannah told her child, "Remain loyal to thy religion and follow in the footsteps of thy brothers."

"Why do you wait? Why do you not kill me as you did my brothers?" This was what Danny was supposed to say.

Instead he heard Miss Sturm's words—*the bravest of all her children!*—echoing loudly in his ears. His speech just wouldn't come.

He clenched his fists. "I want to be like Judah Maccabee," he muttered. "I won't give up without a fight!"

"You bad, bad king!" he yelled suddenly. He fell upon the startled Antiochus with the fury of a warrior.

The mighty king toppled from his throne, and he and Danny tussled and rolled in a heap on the stage floor.

"Stop! Stop, Danny!" Miss Sturm whispered frantically from the wings. "You're supposed to die!" But warrior Danny heard not a word.

The astonished audience watched the struggle silently for a few minutes, not knowing what to make of this strange behavior. Then a hullabaloo broke loose. Everyone jumped up in his seat. Whooping with laughter and excitement, they cheered Danny on. "Attaboy!" "Good for you!" "Give it to him!" "He deserves it!"

Hurriedly the curtain came down. The pianist immediately swung into a Hanukkah song. A few of the children took up the refrain. Then more and more joined. Soon from all over the auditorium roared the triumphant words, *In every generation a hero will come to save the people.*

Strong arms separated the battling Danny from his victim. Red-faced and panting hard, he looked around in distress. What had he done? He'd spoiled the whole play! He began to sob.

All his fellow actors came back and gathered around Danny. They weren't angry—they were full of smiles.

Miss Sturm put her arm around him. "It's all right, all right, Danny. Listen to the audience applauding! They liked your ending much better. Do you hear the words they are singing? 'In every generation a hero will come to save the people!' "

Six Brown Seeds

The room was warm and cozy. The radiators hissed pleasantly, their hot breath shutting the winter out. Miss Sturm beamed at her Sunday school class. "Today we celebrate Hamishah Asar Bishevat," she announced. "It's springtime—"

The children looked at one another. "Springtime!" "But Miss Sturm, it's January!" "It's freezing cold outside!"

Miss Sturm's eyes twinkled. "You didn't let me finish. It's springtime in Israel."

"Oh! In Israel!" The children giggled and wiggled in their seats.

Debbie waved her hand. "What do those words mean, Miss Sturm?"

"Hamishah Asar Bishevat means the fifteenth day of the Hebrew month of Shevat. It's the New Year for the trees."

"Do trees have a New Year?" asked Danny, and everybody laughed.

Miss Sturm smiled and went on. "In olden times, Hamishah Asar Bishevat was tree planting day. For every boy that was born, a cedar tree was planted. That was because cedar trees grow tall and straight and strong. For every girl, a cypress tree, because the cypress is so beautiful and fragrant. All through their lives, the boys and girls tended their own trees carefully. When they grew up and got married, branches of their trees were cut and used to make the wedding canopy."

"Oh, that's nice!" piped up Debbie.

"Yes, it was a lovely custom," agreed Miss Sturm. "But when the Jews were driven from their land, it ended. For hundreds of years, no one took care of the trees. The countryside became bare. Some parts became swampy. These swamps spread sickness and death.

"Then many, many years later, Jewish pioneers came back to the land. They said, 'We must make our country beautiful and healthy once more.' Right away, they began planting trees. First of all the eucalyptus tree, which has long, thick roots to soak up the water. These were planted in the swamps to dry them up.

"Many other trees were planted for fruit, and wood, and shade. Today in Israel, the rocky hills are covered with grass and trees. There are green fields and fine orchards. There are gardens and parks. But there are still many places where trees need to be planted. So in Israel, Hamishah Asar Bishevat again has become the holiday of the trees.

"On this day, all the children gather at their schools. The girls wear flowers and ribbons in their hair. With banners flying, they parade to the fields and forests. Some carry shovels and spades. Others, watering cans and young saplings. While the grown-ups stand around and watch, the children plant their little trees in the ground. They pile up the earth around them and pour water over them.

"Afterwards the children recite poems. They sing happy songs. They form circles and dance gaily around their newly planted trees. It's a wonderfully happy time for all."

"I wish we could do that here," Danny said.

"I wish we could, too," said Miss Sturm. "Perhaps if we lived in the country, we would. But at least we can have a party."

"A party!" "Oh boy!" "A party!" the children cried, hopping up and down in their seats.

Just then, someone knocked on the door. "Here comes the surprise!" Miss Sturm said. The door opened, and in came two older boys. They were carrying trays piled high with assorted fruits and nuts. Carefully, they set them down on Miss Sturm's desk.

"Wow!" "So much fruit!" the children cried in happy excitement.

"On Hamishah Asar Bishevat, we eat the fruits that grow in Israel to show our love for our ancient land," Miss Sturm explained. "Come on, everyone, help yourselves!"

The children didn't need urging. In no time at all everyone was munching happily on grapes, oranges, figs, dates, and almonds.

There was something new on one of the trays. It looked like long, wrinkly, blackish brown sticks. "What's that stuff?" Danny asked.

"The fruit of the carob tree. It grows in Israel," replied Miss Sturm. "Some people call it Saint-John's-bread. We call it bokser."

"It looks like old, dried-up banana skins. Can you eat it?"

"Of course. Anybody want to try some?" Miss Sturm broke off pieces of the bokser and passed them around.

The children bit into them. "It's so hard!" they exclaimed. "But it tastes sweet."

"Be careful of the seeds, children," Miss Sturm warned. "They're hiding inside the bokser in little pockets."

"Here's one," Debbie cried. "It looks just like an apple seed, only bigger."

The children chewed away until all that was left of the bokser was a little pile of brown seeds. Danny examined them curiously. Then he picked out six seeds and put them in his pocket.

When the party was over, Danny hurried home. He crept under his bed and pulled out an old wooden cheese box and a small shovel. Down the stairs he raced and out into the backyard. In another minute he was digging into the hard ground. Soon the box was almost full of damp, dark earth.

Now Danny reached into his pocket and took out the six bokser seeds. Carefully he planted them in the box and covered them with more of the earth.

"This is my own tree planting holiday!" he said, laughing aloud. He set the box down and danced gleefully around it. Soon, he thought, my six brown seeds will grow. Then I'll have six teensy little bokser trees. And someday, when they grow real big, I'll take them back to their home—in Israel.

The Big Sneeze

"Oh, you look so funny!" Mommy's voice ran up and down the hill with laughter.

Danny peeked out from under Daddy's hat. Mommy had stuffed it with paper, so it would fit. "I feel all flippy-floppy!" he cried. Round and round the kitchen he tramped, with Daddy's jacket slapping against his shoes.

"And what's happened to your hands?" exclaimed Mommy. She was laughing so hard, she had to sit down.

Danny held up the dangling coat sleeves. "They're here—inside."

"I'd better pin those sleeves up, or you won't be able to carry the shaloach manot to Grandma and Grandpa."

Oh, thought Danny, if I can't carry the plateful of goodies, there'll be nothing to exchange with Grandpa. After all, that's what shaloach manot means—exchanging gifts. He stood very still while Mommy pinned him up. "I like Purim," he said. "You get all dressed up like somebody else, and you go around visiting everybody."

"Yes, it's a very happy holiday," agreed Mommy. "And for another reason, too. Remember the story about Haman?"

"Uh-huh," Danny nodded. "He was a bad man. A long time ago, he wanted to hang all the Jews in Persia. But God punished Haman. Instead, he got hanged himself."

"Lucky thing, too," replied Mommy, "or maybe there'd be no little Danny today." She gave him a hug. "There now, you're all set."

"Oh, no! First I have to put on my mask!" Danny reminded. Hocus-pocus! All of a sudden, Danny was a rosy-cheeked old man, wearing a long, white beard!

Danny jumped up and down before the mirror. "Grandpa'll never guess who I am!" he cried.

He felt all bouncy with excitement. And when a person felt like that, the only thing to do was to run lickety-split down the block to Grandpa's house. But not now. Now he had to walk slowly like grown-ups did. Otherwise he'd upset the shaloach manot plate.

Danny lifted one corner of the white napkin cover. Mmm! Hamantaschen! (Three-cornered cakes filled with honeyed poppy seeds.) Yummy! And so many nuts, and dates, and raisins too! Danny's tongue slid hungrily over his lips. Maybe if he just took a couple of raisins. . . . No! That wouldn't be right. You mustn't take from someone's present. And anyway, maybe Grandpa would share the goodies with him.

Danny knocked on Grandpa's door. The door opened and there was Grandpa staring at him. "Hrumpf! What can I do for you, sir?"

"How do you do, Mr. Grandpa," Danny replied. "Today is Purim, and I brought you some shaloach manot."

Grandpa bowed. "Welcome, stranger! How nice of you! Come right in. Won't you join my wife and me in a cup of hot tea?"

Grandpa pulled up a chair. "Do sit down, sir. You must be tired from such a long journey."

Just then Grandma came in. "Grandma," said

Grandpa, "this kind gentleman has brought us some shaloach manot."

"Isn't that nice!" Grandma uncovered the plate. "My! Such delicious-looking hamantaschen!" She smiled down on Danny. "Your good wife made them, I suppose!" She took a little bite. "Mmmm! They taste every bit as good as they look. Excuse me while I go make the tea."

Grandpa sat down beside Danny. "Hrumpf!" He looked him up and down. "Such a fine beard you have, sir. You must be a very pious man. Are you perhaps a rabbi?"

Danny just shook his head. He was afraid if he talked, he would start giggling.

"Hmm! You know, sir, you look very familiar. Tell me, do you by any chance come from my hometown—from Vishnitzah?"

"Vishnitzah!" Danny almost laughed out loud at the funny name. He made his voice sound big and gruff. "No. I'm not from there."

"No? I would have sworn you were my wife's cousin. Of course, you do look like a much more learned man than he. Well, I'm honored that you visit us."

Danny shivered with delight. He had been right! Grandpa hadn't guessed who he really was.

Grandpa reached into his vest pocket and took out a tiny enameled box. He pressed a little spring, and the lid popped open. Danny watched as Grandpa put two fingers inside and came up with a pinch of snuff. He breathed it in with big sniffs: first in one nostril, then the other. "Aaah!" Grandpa sighed with great enjoyment. Then he fell to blowing his nose hard in a big red-checkered handkerchief.

"This is a fine snuff! It really clears your nose." Grandpa's eyes twinkled merrily. He held the box out towards Danny. "Please, sir, help yourself. I know that old men like you and me enjoy a pinch of snuff now and then."

Danny pinched some of the wispy brown snuff, just as Grandpa had done. Gingerly he brought the snuff under his mask, and sniffed. In a second, his nose felt all itchy. His eyes watered. Ooh! This was strong stuff! Danny could feel a giant sneeze coming up. From way down deep inside him—up—and up—Danny's head went back—and up!—*"Kerchoo!"* The sneeze exploded like a firecracker. Off flew his mask.

Grandpa guffawed. "Oh my! It's Danny! Can you imagine? My own little grandson, and I never even recognized him! Grandma, come quick! It's Danny!"

Grandma came running, her face all smiles. "You mean that old man was Danny? Well, I never! What a surprise!"

"Yes, it was me all the time!" boasted Danny. "I fooled you, didn't I?"

"You certainly did. Such a wonderful disguise! Grandma, don't you think such a fine show deserves a present?" Grandpa held up a quarter. "Here, Danny, this is for you. And Grandma has something else, too—a shaloach manot plate for you to take back to Mommy and Daddy." Grandpa chuckled. "So, Grandma, where's the tea for the two old men? After all, we have to have something to wash down these wonderful hamantaschen."

Who Has the Matzo?

Grandpa looked different tonight. He was all dressed up. He wore a flowing white robe and a small skullcap with beautiful gold stitching. "Grandpa, you look like a king!" Danny said.

"Tonight I *am* like a king," Grandpa replied, walking slowly to the head of the table. He sank into his armchair piled high with pillows. Leaning back, he smiled. "And Grandma is my queen! Come, sit down everyone, and let the Passover ceremony begin."

"Can I sit next to Grandpa? Can I?" asked Danny.

"Yes, Danny ought to sit there," the older cousins agreed. "Being the youngest, he's going to ask the four questions."

All the uncles and aunts nodded their heads. So Danny sat on Grandpa's left, and Grandma on Grandpa's right.

The Seder table was a marvelous sight. It stretched way out and was covered with a snowy white cloth. The candles sent a golden glow over the special Passover dishes. By each place stood a crystal wine goblet and a copy of the Haggadah (Book of Service).

Everyone hushed. Grandpa began to chant in Hebrew. A little later, he took half a matzo from the plate in the center of the table. "See, Danny," he said, "this is the afikomen. That means it is used at the end of the service." He turned and hid it behind the pillows in his chair. Patting the hiding place, he announced, "Nobody is going to steal it from me tonight. I'll see to that!"

Danny sat up straight in his chair. He didn't want Grandpa to see that he felt all dancy inside. His big brown eyes followed Grandpa's every move.

The service went on. Soon they came to the four questions about the meaning of the Passover holiday. "Well, Danny?" Grandpa encouraged.

Danny wiggled a little. Everybody waited for him to speak. His voice wobbled as he chanted the first question—"Why is this night so different from other nights?" But he finished all four questions without making a single mistake. His mommy and daddy beamed proudly. Danny felt good all over.

Grandpa began to answer Danny's questions. "We were slaves to Pharaoh in Egypt. . . ." Swiftly the pages of the Haggadah were turned as the whole family sang along with him.

Danny couldn't read the Hebrew words of the Haggadah, but he liked looking at its old, little

pictures. He listened to the singsongy chanting of
the grown-ups. Sometimes their voices were
whispery. Other times, they grew loud. But all
the time, Danny kept thinking about the afikomen behind the pillows.

Then it was time for the ceremony of washing
the hands. Grandma brought in a basin of water
and a towel. As she passed by Danny's chair, she
gave him a wink. Was that a signal? Danny won-
dered. His heart made a great big jump.

Grandpa turned his back to Danny. Slowly he poured the water over his hands. Hurry, Danny! a little voice inside him urged. This is a good chance!

Danny's hand shot out, swift as the tongue of a snake. Behind the pillows it dived, and up came the precious piece of matzo. Before anyone could say boo, Danny had tucked it inside his Haggadah. Grandpa didn't seem to notice anything. Danny wanted to laugh out loud, but he kept a straight face.

Now Grandpa gave everyone a portion of bitter herbs to eat, to remind them of the bitter life of the Jews under Pharaoh. The older children screwed up their faces and cried, "Ugh! It's icky!" Danny just swalled his portion quickly and thought—I got the afikomen!

The Haggadahs were laid aside. What a wonderful meal followed! First, hard-boiled eggs, which everyone dipped into salt water. Then, gefilte fish, chicken soup with fluffy matzo dumplings, roast chicken, carrots, and lastly, stewed fruit.

The feasting over, Grandpa started to search behind the pillows. "My afikomen! Somebody stole my afikomen!" he wailed. "Who's the thief?"

Danny clapped his hands, bouncing up and down. "Me, me, Grandpa!" he burst out. "I got it! I got it!"

Grandpa's face crinkled up with smiles. "Well, Danny, what do I have to give you to get my afikomen back?"

Danny didn't hestitate a second. He'd been thinking about the prize for a long time. "A fire engine!" he yelled.

"All right," promised Grandpa. "Now let's have the afikomen. We can't finish the Seder without it."

Danny opened his Haggadah. There lay the afikomen—broken in two!

"Ooh, look what you did!" Danny's cousins exclaimed.

Danny stared down unbelievingly at the two pieces of matzo. Tears swam in his eyes. "It got broke, Grandpa. . . . Now . . . I won't get . . . my present," he blubbered.

Grandpa lifted Danny into his strong arms. "Now, now, Danny," he said. "It doesn't matter. Maybe now that the afikomen is in two pieces, I have to give you two presents instead of one."

At once Danny stopped crying. "You really mean it, Grandpa?" he asked.

Grandpa nodded. "I guess so."

A big grin flashed across Danny's tear-stained face. "Then I want a hook and ladder, also."

Everyone burst into laughter. Danny chuckled all over himself. "Grandpa," he said, "next year, if I catch the afikomen, I'll break it into four pieces! Then you'll have to give me *four* presents!"

Bow and Arrow

"Children," Miss Sturm said, "there'll be no class next Sunday. Instead, we're going on a picnic."

The children bubbled over with cries of delight. "Ooh! A picnic!" "Oh boy, what fun!" "Eats!" "We can roast weenies!"

Miss Sturm's face dimpled. She put up her hands. "Shush, everybody!"

Gradually the class settled down.

"We'll be celebrating the Lag ba-Omer," Miss Sturm continued. "This holiday comes exactly thirty-three days after Passover. I know you're wondering what it has to do with a picnic. But just wait, and you will see.

"First we have to go way, way back to the days when the Romans ruled Palestine. Life was hard. The Romans were cruel. They would not permit the Jews to study the Holy Law and made them pay heavy taxes.

"At this time there lived a great Jewish warrior. His name was Bar Kokhba, which means son of a star. He wanted the people to fight for their freedom. Many stories are told about Bar Kokhba's great strength. It was said he could pull up a tree by its roots while riding by on a horse!"

"Really!" exclaimed Danny, feeling his own muscles.

Miss Sturm smiled and went on. "Now there was also, in the land of Palestine, a great and wise teacher, Rabbi Akiba. 'Join Bar Kokhba in this fight!' he urged the people. And they flocked to Bar Kokhba's side. So began a long and bitter struggle.

"During the war, a plague broke out among Rabbi Akiba's followers. Many thousands died. Then suddenly, on Lag ba-Omer, the plague ended. Also on this day, Bar Kokhba won a great battle.

"For more than three years, the fighting went on. It looked as if the Jews were winning. But the Romans had the strongest armies in the world. When they realized that they might lose, they sent a mighty force into Palestine. The small Jewish army could not hold out against them. They lost, and brave Bar Kokhba was killed.

"Life became worse than ever for the Jews. The Romans passed a law that anyone who studied the Torah would be killed. But the Jews would not give up their learning. Rabbi Akiba and other teachers held classes secretly in the woods.

"This was very dangerous for the young students. Suppose they met Roman soldiers on their way into the forest. Suppose the soldiers would ask, 'Why are you here? Where are you going?'

"So the Jews figured out a way to fool the Romans. The students carried bows and arrows to make it look as if they were going hunting."

"That was pretty smart!" exclaimed Danny. "Did they really fool the Romans?"

"Often they did, Danny. But some of the teachers were caught. Even Rabbi Akiba himself was put to death. Yet the Romans couldn't break the spirit of the Jews. The learning of the Holy Books never stopped!

"And that's why we're having our picnic. We'll go into the woods with bows and arrows, just like those brave students of old. And we'll act out the story of Bar Kokhba."

Danny was so excited, the words came tumbling out like marbles. "And some can be Romans, and some can be Jews? And—and we could have a real fight with bows and arrows . . . ?"

"Just a minute!" Miss Sturm said, laughing. "Remember, it's only to be make-believe fighting. We wouldn't want anyone to get hurt."

"Should we bring along lunch?" interrupted Debbie.

"Of course," replied Miss Sturm. "We can't have a picnic without lunch."

The following Sunday morning, Danny stepped proudly down the street towards Sunday school. A bus already crowded with children stood waiting at the curb. Suddenly a small boy yelled, "Wow! Look at Danny!"

Immediately heads came poking out of the bus windows. "Say! Look at that!" "Hi there, Danny!!" "Look, Miss Sturm!! . . . Look at Danny!"

"What's all the excitement?" Miss Sturm

asked, turning around. There in the doorway stood Danny, dressed like an Indian brave! Bright red and yellow feathers waved gaily above his head and down his back. Shiny red and black streaks of paint zigzagged across his cheeks. In his arms he held a big bow and arrow.

"How! Miss Sturm," he said with a fierce scowl. Putting a hand to his mouth, he let out an Indian war cry. "Whoo—whoo—whoo—whoo—!"

In another minute, the whole busload of children turned into a tribe of whooping Indians.

"Oh my goodness!" Miss Sturm cried.

When at last everyone was quieted down, Miss Sturm asked in a puzzled voice, "Danny, why are you dressed up like an Indian? This isn't an Indian outing. It's a picnic for Lag ba-Omer."

"I know. But you said the Jews in olden times used bows and arrows," Danny reminded.

"Yes, but there were no Indians there."

Patiently Danny tried to explain. "Don't you understand, Miss Sturm? We're going to have a fight between the Romans and the Jews, with bows and arrows and everything. Well, nobody in the whole world could fight with bows and arrows better than the Indians. See?"

Miss Sturm put her hand up to her mouth. She looked at Danny thoughtfully. She seemed to be thinking over what he said. Then she smiled. "Class, wasn't Danny smart to think about all this?"

"Yes, yes!" the children shouted.

"Well, maybe as a reward, he should be Bar Kokhba," suggested Miss Sturm.

"Yes, Danny is Bar Kokhba! Danny is Bar Kokhba!" the children cried out.

Danny Bar Kokhba took his seat in front, right

behind the driver. Folding his arms like an Indian chief, he said, "I wish my friend Bobby was with us. He's got a swell cowboy suit with two six-shooters!"

Mountains of Blintzes

Danny snuggled happily beneath the coverlet. It was story time. He felt comfy-cozy, and drowsy, and full to bursting. "Daddy," he murmured, "Shavuot's a swell holiday, because Mommy always makes lots of cheese blintzes."

"I know," replied Daddy, laughing. "You ate enough blintzes tonight to make a mountain."

Danny grinned and patted his stomach. "It feels like a mountain."

"Want to hear a Shavuot story about mountains?"

"Uh-huh!" Danny flip-flopped on his pillow a

couple of times, getting settled. "All right, Daddy, I'm ready."

"Well, after the Jews left Egypt, they wandered about in the desert for many weeks. One day, they came to a mountain; and it was there, the Bible tells us, that Moses went up to receive the Ten Commandments from God.

"The Comandments are God's laws. They teach us how to be good. To remember this wonderful gift God gave us, we celebrate Shavuot.

"Now, when the mountains first heard that Moses was going to receive the Commandments on a mountaintop, they had begun to quarrel. Each mountain wanted the Law to be given on its peak.

"Mount Tabor spoke up proudly. 'I should be the favored one, for I am the tallest! In the time of Noah, when the great floods came, all you other mountains were covered up by water. Only my head remained safely above!'

"That made Mount Herman very cross. 'Huh! Just being the biggest doesn't count! You've got to do something important! Like me, for instance!'

" 'And what did you do that's so important?' asked Mount Tabor.

"Mount Herman huffed and puffed with pride. 'When the Jews fled from Egypt, the waters of

the Red Sea divided. I got down between the two shores so the Jews could cross over safely.'

"Meanwhile, foxy Mount Carmel plopped itself down beside the sea. 'If I stay right here, I'll surely be the lucky one. For if God wants to give the Law on the sea, then I am on the sea! If on land, then I am also by the land.'

" 'Stuff and nonsense!' shouted the other mountains.

"But little Mount Sinai said nothing. 'I'm so very little,' he sighed. 'Nothing wonderful ever happens to me.'

"Suddenly a voice rang out of heaven. 'The Lord will not choose any of the tall, proud mountains that boast and quarrel. The Lord chooses a humble mountain—Mount Sinai!'

"And that's how little Mount Sinai became the place where the Ten Commandments were given to the Jews."

Danny yawned sleepily. "I'm glad God picked Mount Sinai, Daddy. All the other mountains were so stuck on themselves."

"Goodnight, Danny," Daddy whispered, kissing him.

Danny lay quietly in the soft darkness, thinking about the mountains. All at once his bed started to quiver and shake! Danny sat upright. What was the matter? He stared around. The walls were moving away!

Danny jumped out of bed and raced after them, trying to catch up. It was too late! They were gone!

Danny stopped running. He felt all mixed up. He was outdoors! All around him were big, puffed-up yellow things, and from their tops oozed squashy, creamy stuff. "Ooh! They're blintzes! Mountains and mountains of blintzes!" yelled Danny. But just as he spoke, the shapes changed. No, they were really mountains.

Mountains with faces, all angry and scowling!
Now they were galumphing towards him, groan-
ing and muttering.

"So!" roared one of them. "You think we're
stuck up, do you?"

A second mountain swept its head back and
bellowed, "Look at the size of him! And he dares
to criticize us! Ha! Ha! Ha!!"

"He thinks because he's so full of blintzes, he's
as big as we are!" shouted another.

"Say, Mount Carmel, let's have a little fun

with this blintze boy!" yelled a medium-sized mountain. It bent its crown, and suddenly Danny was lifted high. "Catch!" cried the mountain. WHOOSH! . . . Danny flew through the air. *Smack!* He landed sprawling atop Mount Carmel.

"Oh, please, please, Mister Mountains!" he gasped. No one paid him any attention.

"Your turn, Mount Herman!" screamed Mount Carmel, shaking Danny like a small puppy. WHOOSH! . . . He whirled into space again! *Crash!* He was flat on his face atop Mount Herman!

"This is fun! Send that blintze boy on to me." And Mount Tabor set its peak all ready for the catch.

"Oh, please, Mount Tabor! I'm sorry for what I said. I didn't mean . . ." The only answer the mountains gave was WHOOSH . . . WHOOSH . . . WHOOSH! Danny was being tossed back and forth like a rubber ball.

Danny's stomach began to hurt terribly from all the shaking. "Oh, please! Stop!" he cried.

Suddenly, as he flew over Mount Carmel, Danny spied a low mountain waddling towards him. It had a kind face and was smiling. "Danny," it called out, "I'm Mount Sinai! I'll save you. Quick, land on me! I'll send you straight on home again."

With his heart in his mouth, Danny twisted and turned until he toppled right onto the peak of little Mount Sinai. "Good boy! Now, hold on tight!!" Mount Sinai took a running start. "One—two—three—Let go!"

Danny felt himself falling and falling. From far away, he could hear Mount Sinai calling after him. "Remember, Danny, remember! Someday, come and visit me! Don't forget! Don't forget. . . ."

There was the sound of running feet. A light flashed on. Danny blinked his eyes wonderingly. He was stretched out on the floor of his own bedroom! Over there was his bed, and here were Mommy and Daddy standing over him.

"Danny, you fell out of bed!" Mommy's voice sounded a little alarmed. "Are you hurt?"

"Oh, no!" Danny tried to explain. "I didn't fall. It was Mount Sinai that threw me here."

Mommy and Daddy looked at each other. "Oh, it was only a bad dream," Daddy said.

"I warned him not to eat so many blintzes," Mommy added, laughing.

And they all laughed together.

Tell Me a Story

Danny's nose tingled with delight. "It sure smells good in here!" he exclaimed.

Mommy shut the oven door. "It always does on Fridays." She picked up a bunch of carrots. *Scrape! scrape!* went the knife. "That reminds me of a puzzle," Mommy said. "What holiday is celebrated more often than any other?"

Danny thought and thought. "I don't know, Mommy," he answered finally.

"I'll give you a hint," Mommy said, smiling. "This holiday comes every single week."

Danny grinned. "I know! The Sabbath!"

"That's my smart little boy," Mommy said.
"Come, now, we must hurry. It's almost time for
the holiday to begin."

Mommy spread a snowy white cloth over the
table and laid out her best dishes. In the center,
she stood the gleaming brass candlesticks. She
put two loaves of golden brown hallah at Daddy's
place and covered them with an embroidered hallah cloth. Beside the hallah, she set the silver
kiddush cup (wine cup) and a crystal decanter
of ruby red wine.

Meanwhile, Danny was making himself ready.

First he shined his shoes. Next he shined himself, splashing lots of soapsuds and making fancy noises all the while. Lastly, he put on his good suit. Now he felt fresh and clean and Sabbath-like.

The sun sank from the sky—time to light the Sabbath candles. Danny loved to watch Mommy. She looked so pretty with her shawl covering her hair. He stood very quietly as she held her hands towards the light and recited the blessing.

Soon Daddy returned from synagogue. "Good Sabbath!" he greeted.

"Good Sabbath!" replied Mommy and Danny, and they put up their faces to be kissed.

They sat down to table. Daddy filled the kiddush cup. Lifting it high, he chanted the blessing and took a small sip. Then he uncovered the hallah and cut a big slice for each. Together they made the blessing over the bread.

Now began the eating of the Sabbath meal—gefilte fish, chicken noodle soup, roast chicken and browned potatoes, carrots, and hot tea with the yummiest apple cake ever!

"I'm all stuffed!" Danny sighed contentedly.

Daddy started to sing one of the sweet Sabbath songs that Danny loved so much. He and Mommy sang along, and the room was filled with happy sounds.

Afterwards, Danny hopped into Daddy's lap. "Now tell me a Sabbath story," he said.

"Well," began Daddy, "the story for this week is about a religious cow."

"A religious cow! Whoever heard of that?"

"Well, this one was. She was a fine, healthy cow. She was brown and white, and her eyes were beautiful and wise. And she had a long tail that swished back and forth.

"Her master was very fond of her. He treated

her kindly. And the cow liked him, too. All week long, the cow pulled his plow through the fields. In the spring, she helped with the planting. In the autumn, she helped bring in the harvest. And, of course, all the time she gave her master good, rich milk.

"All this happened long, long ago, when the Jews were the only people who kept the Sabbath. Now, the master was a good Jew. He worked six days of the week. On the seventh, he rested. And so did his cow. Oh, how that cow loved the Sabbath. She'd loll in the fields, nibble away at the grass, and lazily swish her long tail about.

"But then hard times came. The man could no longer keep his cow. He felt very sad when he had to sell her. For the next few days, the cow worked very hard for her new master. He was pleased. Then came the Sabbath.

"Now the new master wasn't Jewish. To him, the Sabbath was like any other day. First thing in the morning, he yoked the cow to his plow. And the cow wouldn't move!

" 'The poor cow must be sick,' he cried. But when he examined her, he found nothing wrong. 'She's just lazy,' he decided. He pulled and he tugged. But the cow wouldn't take even one step.

"The man grew very, very angry. He shouted. He scolded. He even fell to beating her. It was no use. That cow just wouldn't budge. Instead, do you know what she did? She plunked herself right down on the soft grass and lolled there.

"Hopping mad, the man ran to the Jewish farmer. 'I want my money back!' he yelled. 'You sold me a good-for-nothing, lazy cow!'

" 'Oh no!' declared her first master. 'She's a very fine, hardworking cow!'

" 'Bah! Come, and I'll show you how hard-working she is!'

"So they hurried back to where the cow lay. When she saw her old master, she let out a happy moo, and her long tail swished back and forth.

"Bending over, the Jew whispered something

in her ear. At once, the cow arose and moved toward the fields. The new owner was amazed. 'How is it you are able to make her work?— What did you say to her?'

"And the Jew replied, 'I just said, "My dear old friend, now you have a new master. You must obey him. He does not rest on the Sabbath. Therefore you cannot either. . . ." You see, the cow isn't lazy. She's just used to resting on the seventh day, the way we Jews do. But don't worry. Now that she understands, she won't give any more trouble on the Sabbath.'

"The new owner scratched his head in wonderment. Then he said, 'Imagine! A cow knows enough to rest one day of the week while I work all seven days! Well, I won't let a cow be smarter than me! From now on, I shall rest on the Sabbath also!' "

"That's a good story, Daddy," Danny said. "Tell it again!"

Daddy gave Danny a playful pat. "Oh, no you don't, young fellow! It's time for bed."

When Mommy and Daddy had kissed Danny good-night, he murmured sleepily, "Of all the holidays in the whole year, I think the Sabbath is the best. I'm glad it comes every week!"